WHAT HAST THOU IN THE HOUSE

Thoughts from the heart

Author: Patsy Burge

Copyright © 2008 by Patsy Burge

What Hast Thou In The House
Thoughts from the heart
by Patsy Burge

Printed in the United States of America

ISBN 978-1-60647-710-6

All rights reserved solely by the author. The author guarantees all contents are original and do not infringe upon the legal rights of any other person or work. No part of this book may be reproduced in any form without the permission of the author. The views expressed in this book are not necessarily those of the publisher.

Unless otherwise indicated, Bible quotations are taken from The King James Version.

www.xulonpress.com

Thanks

Thanks to my elder daughter for showing me how much love one child could generate. I never knew I could have so much compassion and patience with anyone until you entered this world. You were a dream child, always striving to please, and you seldom got into trouble.

Thanks for creating the title of this book for me. Since your childhood antics do not pepper the pages as numerously as those of your little sister's antics, I am thrilled that your title contribution is displayed on the front cover. You were always afraid you might do something wrong, where your little sis was afraid she might <u>not</u>! I do not want to seem partial, but her sassy mouth provided more fodder for stories than your humble character. You did tell me that you knew it was hard for me to write about such a "perfect" child, but just remember your father said he had an <u>entire</u> book about "a perfect child,"- Jesus!

You are blessed with musical talent for entertaining family and friends. God has used your piano playing to enhance the church services and bless your mother's heart. As the elder child, you set a wonderful example for your sister to follow, and I am so thankful to be your mother!

Thanks to my younger daughter for proving I could love another little bundle of joy with as much passion. I feared I could not love as deeply the second time, but God proved

He could multiply my loving power and not diminish the feelings I had for my first child. You brought more laughter into our home than we thought possible, and your antics never ceased. We marveled how one person could be so hilarious. You never ran out of new material to use in your comedy. You are truly a gift from God!

Your juggling college and work (thus far maintaining a 4.0) demonstrates your devotion to reaching for the stars. I feel you have a bright future if you continue to stay close to the Lord.

Both of you were saved within twenty-four hours and were baptized together. No greater blessing could be bestowed upon parents! God has blessed us abundantly and I hope we are as grateful as we should be to Him.

Thanks to my Heavenly Father for choosing me to be your mother! He could have given me any child He desired, but he chose the best two little girls in the world for me to love and cherish. It was through His mercy that I was given the privilege to write and share stories from your childhood.

Thanks to my dear husband Clay who stood by me and encouraged me through the writing of this book. You believed I had the ability to complete the task even when I found myself doubting. Thanks for your devotion and the years of being the best father our little girls could ever want.

Thanks to my sister Beth Haden and my high school English teacher Mrs. Ilean Allen for proofreading this manuscript.

Thanks to Tara Burge for listening to my endless story ideas and forwarding me the encouraging email that introduced me to the publisher of this book.

STILL LEARNING

The more I learn about life, the more I realize how little I know. I only have a vague concept of what there is to be learned before full maturity can be achieved. Each day brings new problems and experiences that either help promote growth and wisdom or failure and defeat. This daily process will continue until death, since new guidance is needed for each path we travel and each stage of life through which we pass.

I homeschooled my two daughters from kindergarten through twelfth grade; I probably learned more than they did. Since I was responsible for their education and understood the seriousness of poor quality teaching, I leaned toward strict rules and constant guidance. I realized that it was my responsibility to guide their young minds and to lead their lives toward success or failure. This learning process was a relationship-building time for the girls and me. It caused me to dig deeper to assure myself that they would be armed with the proper ammunition with which to greet the future college years and working world.

This was the period in my life when my interest in storytelling grew. I took different real-life scenarios and transformed them into stories (they called it preaching) to hold the attention of my daughters and to teach a life lesson.

However, I always seemed to be instructing myself, because my stories tended to magnify my failures and made me strive to improve my parenting skills.

Both of my girls are now grown, but I am still learning from them. Every new task in our lives broadens our knowledge. When we stop growing in knowledge, we will be dying. Therefore, my motto is, "He who thinks he knows it all knows nothing."

FIFTY WHITE CROSSES

Our church took part in a display in honor of all aborted babies. I volunteered to paint the crosses that had been pre-assembled and given to the church. It took hours of painting to cover that great number of crosses. I kept thinking how this wood was being used to recognize all the innocent babies who had lost their lives through abortion. Every reminder that can be placed in a public area should be erected, because America is killing a generation of children that will stand as a witness against us in heaven.

This cross painting project caused me to have a straight talk with my girls. They knew the teachings we had instilled in them, but did they know that we would accept their mistakes, and, with God's help, raise any child that they brought into this world? Maybe the fear of facing angry parents has caused the abortion count to escalate. Have we only told them what not to do and never shown them we can show acceptance and love even if they do make mistakes?

The following poem came to me during the hours that I spent painting. I could picture children meeting their mothers for the first time at judgment and wondered what their mothers would tell them. Would they explain that they were trying to hide their pregnancy from their parents? Lord, please forbid that I would ever be the cause of an unborn baby's death!

HOLD ME MOM

I have no memory of the day my life was taken from me.
But God didn't think I was a nuisance, He said with Him
   I'd be.
He cleaned me up, held me close, and said with Him I'd
   stay.
He said, "Don't cry, my child; you'll see Mom resurrection
   day."
I never toddled on unsure feet and fell into your arms,
But I fell into the arms of God when my embryo was
   harmed.
Mom, when you get to heaven, you'll be shocked to see
   me.
God says I'm a beautiful child with a delightful
   personality.
You'll be surprised after you squelched my life and
   onward trod.
Though I've never slept in your arms, I've slept in the
   arms of God.
Mom, when I see you, will you have my smile?
Jesus says mine lights my face and shows no trace of
   guile.
Here, there is no hatred or grudges, so I'm not mad with
   you.

What Hast Thou In The House

But I do wonder what Earth is like... like running and playing too.
I'm enjoying it here, but I would love to visit you a while.
For once, I'd have a mom with whom to share a smile.
I would have loved to climb mountains and swim in streams,
But life up here is better than any worldly dream.
Oh, Mom, please catch me a butterfly in a jar of fresh sun-kissed air.
I'd surely like to experience some of the things you have down there.
Do I have sisters and brothers? Would I have had friends there too?
Or were they taken before birth, so their moms could start life anew?
Mom, I would have tried to make you proud and bring you joy each day.
But some things can never be, since our bodies parted ways.
What would I have contributed to society, a cure for cancer you guess?
I may have even brought you shame and ruined your life-long quest.
Oh, Mom, I'm looking forward to meeting you! I'm excited as can be.
I've never seen anyone who really resembles me.
The day my little heart was stopped, I came here to stay.
But, Mom, I'm longing for a hug from you on resurrection day!

WHAT HAST THOU IN THE HOUSE

In II Kings 4:1-7 we learn of a woman who was in so much debt that her sons were being taken as bondmen. She came to Elisha, the prophet of God, and requested his advice. He simply asked her, "What hast thou in the house?" She answered, "Thine handmaid hath not any thing in the house, save a pot of oil." Notice he asked what she had and not what could she get. The story continues with her pouring the oil into borrowed vessels, filling them, and never running out of the small amount of oil with which she started. God provided enough oil from what she already had to fill enough vessels to pay her debt. Her only requirements were to borrow vessels to fill and sell the oil. She used something God had already blessed her with, a small amount of oil, and never depleted the supply.

When God calls us into His service, He uses what he has blessed us to have. He does not require that we become as our fellow man. He has granted us talents when creating us. We may need to polish our talents and enhance our abilities to be of our best service to Him, but we already possess the foundation needed. We cannot be like others whom we admire. They were given a specific personality for a special service, where we are given what is required to fill the capacity God has for us.

There are people whom I admire and long to emulate. They seem to have all the blessings and talents poured into one being. Then I remember that God said that to whom much was given, much would be required. I do not need more gifts since I probably do not honor God with those He has already blessed me to have.

I spend time contemplating the exact purpose of my life. Am I doing what I was put here to accomplish? Am I too blind to see the talents already given? Every Christian must come to the realization that no one can tell him what God's plan is for his life. We all need to meditate on the question, "What hast thou in the house?"

ALWAYS PREPARED

Our young children absorb more information in the church services than we realize. My younger daughter did not tell me until she was older that when she was a small child she had worried about the Lord's return to earth. When it came bath time she rushed to finish and get dressed just in case God chose that moment to call us home. She did not want to go to heaven naked! She also kept, underneath the edge of her bed, a little pink "Going to Grandma's" sack, packed with extra underwear. Her intentions were to grab it if He came during the night! It really hurt me when I realized she had gotten that worried about something I did not realize she understood. Instead of it being a consolation that she would be in a better place, she worried about what she would wear. That really does sound like a female.

After she told me about her childish fears, I wondered if she were really more in tune with God than I had been. She had striven to be prepared whether He came day or night; I, in turn, wondered how often the subject ever crossed my mind during those same years. Her preparations might have been from childish fear, but mature Christians should be considering the real fear of being caught without our spiritual clothing in place. Are we clothed in the assurance that our families are saved and ready to meet the Master? Are we

What Hast Thou In The House

covered in the blanket of love for our fellow man? Do we have rewards for good deeds, packed and waiting in heaven for us to receive when He comes?

There are times I dwell on this subject, but I usually think of its taking place in the future. Who awakens in the morning and thinks, "Today is the day"? We are planning future events with no thought that several of the members of the planned events may be left crying on earth and wondering what has happened to their friends. Why have they suddenly left?

Will cars crash because of no driver? Will homes burn where stoves were left cooking? Will a classroom of students disappear right before a teacher's eyes? I have no idea what will happen when we leave, but I know it will be horrible for all left behind.

Today, let us start covering our carnal beings with a spiritual cloak to hide the nakedness of our indifferent attitudes toward the imminent return of Jesus. We all want to be found clothed in righteousness, ready, watching, and waiting.

LET'S PLAY BALL

Our daughters have always had a special love for softball. If they hear the crack of a bat, they find the game and ask to play. They had been part of a group that assembled on Sunday evenings at my brother's ball field, but this group had temporarily disbanded, due to school, jobs, and life in general, but, on this Sunday, several had agreed to resume their spirited competition. This group is not just children. Several "older" adults, who have to rub down with medicine after each game, still are front and center when the first ball is pitched.

One of the players, who is in his fifties, seemed to enjoy joking with my daughters. There was always friendly gibing among them, if they were in hearing distance of each other. This "older" player threw a ball to get my daughter out, but it made contact with her head. I was not present, but I was told she went to the ground trying to bite back the tears. She yelled to him, "You're not as good as you used to be. You're losing power in that arm." She did not want him to know she was hurting, so she had turned it into a joke.

About an hour later, my husband Clay and I were working constantly to keep her awake, so we loaded up and rushed to the emergency room. After a scan, a young doctor, who had detected my daughter's dry sense of humor, stated that the good news was they had found a brain in her head after all! He gave us instructions; we were dismissed.

I could not settle down that night. I kept thinking how different it all could have ended. I wrote the following letter and taped it to the bathroom mirror, so she could read it the next morning and maybe realize how blessed we had been.

COUNTING BLESSINGS

Thank you, Lord, for blessing me to have a CAT scan bill and an ER fee charged to our account. Thanks for the hours I am sitting up tonight waiting to arouse my daughter from her sleep to make certain she is conscious. Thanks for letting me have the dirt prints of her cleats to mop from the living room floor. It could have all been so different!

If it were not for your mercy, the bills could be for funeral costs, the sleepless night could be from crying over her death, and these footprints could be the last she ever made. Thanks, Lord, for letting this softball blow to her head remind me once more of how richly we are blessed.

Lord, tonight when I awaken her for her health check, I'll give her an extra big hug and wipe the tears from my eyes before resting my head once more in Your lap of mercy.

PRAY FOR THE BUTTERFLY

I always need to exercise, so on this particular day I had chose to bike ride down an old roadbed from yesteryear made visible only by rutted patches of gravel and grass. I bounced along drinking in the beauty of the soybean fields with their foliage bowing in the wind and dancing in the southern sunshine. Suddenly this view was overshadowed by a mass of yellow that caught my attention. In front of me, resting on the puddles of water among the grassy ruts, were hundreds and hundreds of beautiful, yellow butterflies!

I could never disturb such grandeur! I wanted to capture this on film, so I rushed home for my camera, but I found no butterflies when I returned. It was as though this was a precious moment meant only for me! I had to picture it in my mind and share this picture through words instead of pixels.

I shared this sighting with my husband, and his explanation gave me the most awesome insight into the Christian life! He said these butterflies could have emerged from the worms that had fed on the fields of soybeans. They had hatched and started their adult life at the same field they had fed on and destroyed. A beautiful thought took shape in my mind. The butterflies were no longer being sprayed with poison to protect the plants from being eaten. They were now a thing of beauty that had emerged from a cocoon of change. Now they could spread pollen to help plants produce seed and fruit. No longer will they destroy, but they are now an asset.

The same can be done with our lives. It does not matter what sins we have committed, because God always has the power to poison the sin and place us in a cocoon of change. We can then grow and mature and be useful in God's service. The beauty of Jesus in our lives will shine through and attract the attention of the world, drawing others to Christ and causing others to want to be more like us. What we have received, they, too, will want.

This worm was the destroyer that turned into a beautiful, colorful creature. This could represent a Christian's mistakes being replaced with forgiveness and love.

The cocoon is the transformation period from ugly sin to a beautiful God-inspired life. It represents a quiet time of fetal rolling up in sorrow, listening, and waiting on God to make the difference. This transformation period begins when one is willing and ready to turn to God. It is a time of rebuilding, growing, and searching for God's plan in one's life.

The butterfly is the result of this wonderful process, a matured and changed person that is breathtakingly beautiful in God's service.

A serious mistake in one's life does not have to define forever who that person is. When one leaves the mistake behind, with God's help, that person can become something beautiful and useful. Many, who have been bogged down in sin or mistakes in life, rely on encouragement from fellow Christians to help produce this transformation. So, never push the worm down, always encourage the cocoon, and pray that the butterfly can be useful in God's service.

WHAT DID I SAY

My mother and daddy visited a doctor in town. At a specific time, my daddy had to leave for another engagement although Mother had not completed her office visit. Daddy called me to come and take his place in the waiting room, so Mother would have a ride home. There was one problem; Clay had taken the radiator from my car to have it cleaned and repaired. Daddy told me to walk to his house and get Mother's car for the trip. So on this hot July day, I rushed through the woods to their house, got her car, which was equipped with all the bells and whistles, and started the thirty-five minute drive to town.

After the long walk through the woods, I needed the air conditioner on max, but something did not seem right; my seat was getting hotter and hotter. It slowly dawned on me that I had heard something about this car coming equipped with a seat heater, but how had I turned it on? I am much taller than my mother, so I had adjusted the seat, moved the steering wheel, set the mirrors, and who knows what else. I punched every button from the lights, radio, mirror, seat, clock, air conditioner, horn ...you name it, and I punched it trying to find the off button. Nothing would turn off this seat heater! My clothes were getting wetter and wetter, and I kept turning up the air and punching buttons.

What Hast Thou In The House

A small service station is located twelve minutes from my driveway. I quickly decided to pay the owner a visit and beg for help. I did not have time to lose, but I could not ride much longer in the hot seat. I drove up to the front where he and his wife were sitting on a bench, hurriedly slid out of the car and asked, "Sir, can you help me? My seat is so hot!"

I knew he gave me a strange look, so I repeated my request so he would understand it was urgent. He still gave me a strange look, so I said, "Just feel and see!"

About this time I realized what I said was not exactly what I meant! I stammered and tried to straighten out the situation. "Please check my CAR seat," I said. "There is a heater in it and I cannot turn it off."

"I have never heard of such a thing," was his reply.

His wife spoke up; and yes, she had heard of a seat heater before, so we all quickly started pushing more buttons. After several minutes, his wife found the switch located right under the seat adjustment that I had used earlier. One click and the hot seat began to cool.

Though I do go to that service station occasionally to buy gas or update my inspection sticker, I have never again discussed this incident with them. I still wonder what he thought when I slid out of the car and requested his help.

I have told my friends this story, and they found it very funny, but at that moment, I was too embarrassed to see the humor. Yes, I made a safe trip and retrieved my mom, and, no, I have never driven that car again.

How many times do we speak before we consider how our words will be perceived? Have we uttered words that we later wished we could take back? We have a saying at our house that we should make our words sweet in case we have to later eat them.

The more we pray and the closer we are to God, the better we will be able to control our tongues and injure less people. I know my slip of the tongue was not a permanent disgrace.

I feel sure the service station owner has laughed about the incident many times, or it may have never crossed his mind again. Whatever he may have thought does not change the fact that I truly stuck my foot in my mouth that day.

WHAT IS NORMAL?

What is normal for a certain type of attire, hairstyle, home size, food, drink, or transportation mode? We all criticize others for not being normal (as we are), but what is the basic criteria for normal? Every nation of people views normal as being like themselves. Therefore, the only foundation to build upon for normal would be the Bible. The boundaries and borders that the Bible gives are our only guidelines to what is normal.

My personal view of normal would be nothing in excess. Too little pride and you may become slothful with your personal upkeep. Too much pride and you may spend extravagantly on upkeep.

Too little food and you become malnourished. Too much food and you become obese.

Too little money and you may steal or beg. Too much money and you may be wasteful.

Too little exercise and you may become weak and out of shape. Too much exercise and you may become obsessed with muscles.

Too little medicine and you may die. Too much medicine and you may die.

The next time you start to condemn someone for not being normal, remember with whom you are comparing him. If you are comparing him to yourself, well, YOU may not be normal.

UNITY

Unity provides the harmony for a nation, race, community, or family. This one small word is powerful enough to transform turmoil into peace. It holds the power to end wars, restore oneness in communities, and heal friendships. Unity is brought to fruition through sacrifice of one's personal desires. A selfish desire to stand out and be noticed will hinder unity.

A building under construction may have all the materials stacked on the construction site, but until they are joined together to form the structure, there is no unified shelter. A pile of lumber has no resemblance to the finished building it is intended to construct. Shingles, felt, concrete, electrical wires, nails, sheetrock, reinforcement steel bars, air ducts, plumbing pipes, appliances, flooring, paint, windows, doors, studs, trusses, and numerous other supplies must be united in harmony for a construction to be completed successfully. These supplies stacked on a job site do not equal a shelter. All the parts are there, but these supplies must be unified before a building can be made useful.

The unity of America is eroding! All the parts that are needed to complete a harmoniously perfect nation are at our fingertips. The task of bringing the divided segments together appears overwhelming, but all things are possible through prayer and belief in God. According to the Bible, perfect unity will not be achieved until God returns and puts evil under His feet. This does not give us the "go home free" pass to stop praying and doing what God places on our hearts. Each prayer, made in sincerity to God, will be heard. Just because things will not be perfect until Jesus comes, we are not released from our duty to pray for unity in our nation.

THE SOUNDTRACK OF LIFE

I was asked by my younger daughter what the music of my life's soundtrack would be if it were made into a recording. What a powerful question! I had never considered a life to be a musical rendition. It would seem logical that if one were a person who portrays anger and hate, one's music would not be as soothing as that of one who lived his or her life calm and close to God.

A loving mother's music could be a soft, caressing sound that soothes fears and calms jangled nerves. A father's music could be robust and assuring, with perfectly placed drumbeats, a rhythm intended to keep one's steps sure and sharp.

Consider your actions. Would your music be a positive or negative sound? Have you led a life of chaos and fear; have you led a life of love and contentment? If only we were privileged to hear the sound of our life, we could navigate towards making positive the lasting impressions that we stamp upon our children's minds.

THE HOURGLASS

If at the time of one's birth an hourglass were issued to him holding the appropriate quantity of sand to span his life, he would have the ability to estimate the number of years granted to him on earth. Each day he could watch as the grains of his life slowly squeezed through the vessel of time. The awareness of fleeing hours and opportunities would haunt his thoughts.

We are not given a measurement of our days, but we are told that death is coming to all. Since we do not have a constant reminder such as the dripping of the sand of our days into an hourglass, we become complacent and negligent in considering the uncertainty of tomorrow. One lives as though he has time to waste, not thinking that today could be the last chance he has to mend the broken threads of friendship, love his family, live for God, and, most importantly, consider his eternity.

Why does man have no measurement of his days? I believe he would not enjoy the days granted if he knew his future. The uncertainty of his death date allows him to enjoy today and plan for tomorrow without constantly watching his life ebb away. The knowledge of his children's impending death date would rob him of the spontaneous pleasure he feels while yearning for the maturing child to advance from crawling to graduation from school.

There could be some positive effects from knowing the number of one's days. One would be more aware of the passage of time and this alone could influence one to strive to do his best.

Humankind should be thankful that God planned his life span and gave him no knowledge of this timetable. This uncertainty allows man to be free to follow his chosen path, not knowing if death will prevent its completion. If the hourglass showing his impending death loomed as an ornament on his mantel, man would live in misery as the sands of his time slipped away.

STOWAWAYS

While making my beauty supply delivery rounds, I generally listen to a couple of talk shows on the radio. On this particular day, I kept hearing sounds of birds chirping in the background while the shows were airing. I asked my husband if he had listened to the shows, and he had, but no, he had not noticed the new outdoor sounds they had added. I just thought the road noises in his truck probably drowned out the chirps or that he had not paid close attention.

The next day I again loaded my supplies and cranked my van to leave and again I heard the bird sounds, but the radio was OFF! Since we have a nest of birds hatching in our front porch ferns, I figured one had been trapped inside the van. I asked my husband to search the vehicle.

My dear husband had to remove the side panel from the rear interior wall to reach the noise. There to our dismay was an entire family of baby rats! Now, I HATE RATS, so I literally went bananas when I realized I had hauled them all over town!

The rat nest was removed, the babies were removed, the van was sprayed, and I still did not want to drive. I jumped each time the vehicle made a different sound. I could just feel something crawling up my legs! I was so terrified all day while driving that I had muscle spasms in my neck and legs that night.

What is the moral to this story? I am not sure, but maybe it is "If you don't like rats, don't drive the ratmobile!" That is the new name for my van.

WHAT IS NEXT?

Yesterday tried my patience! Did I take it calmly? Only God knows my heart, so I seriously cannot say for sure. I do know that everything seemed to go south. The problems built to a peak by sunset. First, we were told that our daughter's tuition was due, in full, in two weeks; the college had no payment plan. Second, we had sold a cow to pay the bill for a new transmission we had put in our van, but the cow was too small or the price was too low; I am not sure which. More money was needed. Third, the air conditioner unit for our house decided to die just as we were leaving for a meeting. Forth, the new transmission in our van stopped working while we were on our way to a Sunday school meeting in the next town.

As my husband and I drove to the meeting in his work truck, we discussed the meaning of so many trials in one day. Were we to receive a lesson from this? Was there overlooked wrong in our lives? Was God trying to get our attention? I even discussed these questions with our friends at the meeting. The answer I received from them was not an answer I had considered! Maybe God was not punishing us at all; it could be the problems were normal occurrences. Everyone has his share of bills and breakdowns. No one has a life of ease.

What Hast Thou In The House

We returned home during a rainstorm and drove to our humble home, which still had no air conditioning. My husband suggested we get the mail since the mailbox leaked. In the box was a check from my husband's employment, covering the tuition for my daughter's college and the money for the books that we had already purchased. Thank God! The money had been there all day in the damp box just waiting for the right moment to ease our worries. Not only was there enough money to pay for the college tuition, but also enough to pay the remainder of the transmission cost. We went to bed content that God was still on His throne and smiling down on His children.

We raised the windows to let in the breeze, and the sound of gentle falling rain could be heard hitting against the panes. I lay in bed comfortable and sheltered; I then realized the meaning of the day. When everything is going great, we have less need to look up; we become complacent and forget how much we are blessed. I lay in bed thanking God for a home, which kept me sheltered from the rain. My home might not be the best home in the area, but it is far better than I deserve. Even though all seemed to have gone wrong, we still had our health, home, friends, and most of all our fellowship with God. What had seemed to be a day of problems and worries transformed into a time of apologies to God, and a time to thank Him for the many blessings that I take for granted each day.

This was the first night that the temperature had not soared. I lay in bed comfortable and cozy, while listening to the rain and thanking God for His sweet reminder that He is still in control. I no longer felt the trials were punishment for wrongs committed, but the trials were a gentle reminder always to pray when times are good or bad. God is in control at all times and ready and waiting for me to open my heart and receive the many blessings that He has in store for me.

My troubles and trials pale in comparison to the sorrows that others have faced. I see others suffer, but somehow I still have a tendency to complain when minor problems arise in my life. As long as I have my family and health, Lord, help me remember that I still have it all.

TO STARVE OR TO FEED

Some things in life are to be fed and some are to be starved. It is your decision which to nurture. A child should receive all the spiritual food and food of encouragement that a parent can feed him, but the food of fear and suppression should never enter his digestive system. If the nourishment is to be of the most benefit, one should add vitamins to the diet. This would be a form of fertilizer to stoke the body and produce the healthiest child.

Children should never be fed gossip. This food corrupts their minds and produces critical and judgmental individuals. If children are starved of gossip, they will grow to be positive individuals who respect others and possess abundant love. If gossip is made available through the friends your child keeps, poison the seeds immediately. A poisoned seed has less chance of taking hold in a child's heart and corrupting his thoughts. Teach him that he is to set an example for his friends and not to follow them in their wrong.

Plants respond to the amount of love you give to them. Without a diet of water, sun, and fertilizer, the plants would become weak and die. Always keep the weeds pulled from the roots of plants, so they will not lose the nourishment you intended for them to receive, since the unrestrained weeds will thrive and eventually choke out the wanted plants. The same is true for rearing our children. If we plant seeds of love, understanding, and patience instead of seeds of hate, gossip, and criticism, our chances are much greater for rearing a well-adjusted citizen who will be respected by God and man.

Always feed a diet of good seeds to our children. Remember to poison the enemy weeds, and to water our youth with love and security.

TO BEFRIEND A CHILD

If you befriend one child in your lifetime and help to mold his life toward the betterment, what a great accomplishment you have achieved! You may have laid the foundation for him to be open to God's service and to accept the Lord in his life. You may have saved future families from tears over an act of murder this child would commit without past influences to lean upon.

If you intervene and help mold the thoughts or conscience of one child, you may have saved thousands by giving the world one less terrorist! If someone could have touched Osama Bin Laden's life and changed his course, would the towers still be standing and would all his victims still be alive?

Think of Hitler, Mussolini, Sadam Hussein....

God is the only one who knows what your Godly friendship with a child may help to prevent. The world might be saved from terror or tears, or a mom may still have her family alive, and you only touched the life of ONE child!

ALWAYS remember to be kind to the little tots. You may be making a lasting impression on someone who will be powerful as an adult or...on the doctor who will set your hip after you have fallen in a nursing home!

SNAP JUDGMENT

This week I made a trip to our local shopping center and encountered a woman standing beside her car while taking the last few drags on her cigarette. The intense heat outside would have made most people dash into their vehicle and turn on the cooling, but, no, she needed that last buzz before hitting the road. My mind raced with judgment. Her small child was sitting in the hot car without the motor running. Who could be that hardhearted?

I muttered underneath my breath as I drove away. "What does it take to be that crazy? She is killing herself one drag at a time. There is nothing healthy about this situation. A small child was watching her as she slowly harmed herself! The hot car was no place to leave a child while she mindlessly enjoyed one more puff! That money could have been put to better use." Then it dawned on me. I am now driving out of Wal-Mart's parking lot to get a mocha at the local coffee shop. Now, who has the worst hang-up? I am slightly overweight. Each time I drink mocha, I begin to smother just a little, not enough to scare me, but just enough to let me know I need to stop. I have to purchase one each time I get near the coffee shop. Surely, one more mocha will not really make that much difference.

I still drove over and made my purchase. My thoughts did not deter me from my mission. The mocha tasted just as good as the last one I had drunk. The price had not been reduced. I smothered just as much as usual. I probably gained just an ounce or two, but who is counting? I drew consolation from the knowledge that no child was sitting waiting for me, no mocha has a warning posted on the side, and I do not drink hourly or daily.

Human minds always race to make their mistakes appear less dangerous than the mistakes of others. Our minds reflect our actions in the best light. Our wrongs are never as great as the wrongs of others whom we are watching. The next time I jump to judgment, I need to look at myself. After I clean the faults from around my own heart's door, I will probably be too tired to worry about what someone else is doing.

KEYS

It is so amazing how something as small and inexpensive as a key can unlock the heaviest doors and grant entrance into the largest buildings. In life, keys unlock different doors. These doors are not physical entrances into which one may enter. These are the doors to one's heart.

A single word can be the key to unlock the turmoil that is trapped within one's soul. The simple word *sorry* can begin a healing that replaces the festering of hurt inside one's heart. Years of feeling worthless and unloved can be replaced with the jubilant warmth of hope and acceptance. This one simple word releases waves of emotions that have been suppressed and swings the rusty hinges that trapped one's turmoil.

The enunciation of this word is not complex; it is the spirit in which the apology is delivered that seems hard to muster. Humans magnify the importance of always being right. They never seem to believe they are capable of making a mistake. This one belief has broken many fellowships and alienated family members from their loved ones.

I am sorry is not the only phrase that is difficult to utter. Consider the phrase *thank you* and the power it possesses. These tiny words carry so much weight and are capable of lifting a tremendous load from one's heart, so why do we refuse to use them? One who does not find it disturbing to admit his faults or show appreciation for those who have been of assistance in some small way possesses the valuable keys to the private well-being of others.

We all should learn the importance of these tiny inexpensive keys that can alleviate the agony of hurt and depression. These keys are so easy to use and are offered free of charge to all humankind. So, keep your ring of keys, to home and heart, at your fingertips. They could save you many hours of being locked from the doors of friendship and happiness.

JUST ONE MATCH

Have you ever been plunged into darkness from a power outage? Now, picture that same dark room with just one lit match. Everyone's eyes would turn to the only spot of light that broke through the darkness. A Christian's life could give the same illumination in this dark world as the match gave in the dark room.

People think one life cannot make a difference. Well, they should think again. It took one man named David to free Israel from Goliath, one man named Noah to build the ark and save humankind from destruction, one man named Moses to lead the children of Israel from Egypt, and one woman named Mary to bring Jesus into the world. All these brave people had empowerment from above to perform these tasks. They only had to be willing to let God use their lives when the need presented itself.

Every individual can make a difference in his surroundings. One small deed can mushroom and pass from person to person until the transformation has reached beyond human imagination. The smallest deeds are sometimes the most valuable. A kind word could give someone a reason to live and prevent a suicide. One never knows the state of another person's mental health. One's kind word could even cause others to emulate his actions.

One will never know until judgment what impact he has had on his fellow man. Humanity may never comprehend the small changes one can set into motion by his constant living for God. The deeds that God executes through a person will not return unto Him void.

One Christian, who is living for God, certainly can stand out from the general crowd. His response to evil can be that match in the darkest room. All eyes can be focused upon him as the brightness of Jesus shines through. It pays to be different. A lit match can safely lead others through unfamiliar territory. It can prevent tragedy and destruction by illuminating a pathway to the exit door.

We can be this one match. We can be the light that pierces the darkness and glows with love and Godly understanding. We can be the people God chooses to build an ark of love, wipe the tears, give of our money, work with missions, or just bow our heads in earnest prayer to Him.

YOU NEVER MENTIONED HIM

In August 2008, while watching the Olympics in China, I observed the crowded stadium rocking with cheers. I wondered, what if the Lord came back right now? How many of these seats would vacate? How many cheers would transform to screams of fear? Would enough members of the crowd be saved and leave for heaven for them to realize something had taken place? I do not know anyone's heart but my own, so I have no estimate of how many people will leave the ground when God calls his children home.

A song surmises what might take place at the final judgment when the lost are brought before God's White Throne. It states that someone may cry out to those they knew on earth and say, "You never mentioned Him to me, You helped me not the light to see; You met me day by day and knew I was astray, Yet never mentioned Him to me."* Will our friends and acquaintances look at us at the judgment, with tears streaming down their faces, and ask why we did not tell them about the Lord so they too could be saved from eternal destruction in hell? I am truly afraid several can say this to me. I shop and know the cashiers by name. We exchange comments on everything from weather to family, but I still walk away and do not mention the most important subject, the only subject that has eternal value, the only subject that determines if their final destination is in the arms of God or in the eternal flames of hell.

My mind scans my school friends, my neighbors, my work friends, my children's friends, and the pedestrians I speak with when shopping. Why is it so hard to bring up the eternal destination of their soul? If I knew they were going to be robbed or harmed, I would be compelled to warn them, but mentioning God's salvation plan is just too hard to do. This plan will shield them from eternal destruction, not just immediate danger.

I pray that I will become more emboldened in God's work and have the ability to talk with my fellow man about his final destination. I always fear he will differ with me and dismiss me as too religious. Does it really matter if he does? Feeling rejected for doing something good is far better than feeling responsible for not doing anything at all.

*Song excerpt - "You Never Mentioned Him to Me" written by J. W. Gaines and James Rowe

INNER JOY

What brings us joy? When we are all alone, do we have a sense of dread or depression? We should NEVER allow another person to be our source of happiness, because humans can always stumble and disappoint. If we are drawing our happiness from the actions or the devotion of another person, we are making a sad mistake. Our happiness should come from within.

In the dark of night or the brightness of day, we must live with ourselves. We do not have the ability to flee from ourselves without the use of drugs or other mind-altering aids. As long as we are conscious, we must deal with our thoughts and actions. A pure heart before God brings the most joy. The knowledge that God hears our prayers when we talk with Him is enough to bring tears of joy. In the same manner, a dirty conscience weighs heavily on our heart, causing tears and short tempers. The purer our heart grows, the happier our outward countenance will appear.

There are some instances when we carry a heavy burden caused by a loved one's misdeeds or a personal loss; this brings heaviness to our heart, but it does not kill our inner joy. The true joy, buried within our heart, cannot be erased. The joy we acquire through living for God not only lives within our heart on earth but will also be a treasure stored in heaven.

If we depend on another person to supply our happiness, be it a husband, child, friend, or parent, we are surrendering the control of our wellbeing to another individual. All humankind is capable of failure. Do we really want a carnal being to control our life?

If this should happen to us, we should seek guidance from God. He is the only one who can guide us toward the inner personal happiness we deserve. We should find an activity or hobby to fill the void in our life. We could always volunteer to help others. This alone would brighten our spirits and satiate our soul.

Dependency of any nature is hard to relinquish, and this dependency of misguided happiness will not be immediately transferred. Patience with ourselves must be practiced. Keeping a busy schedule is also helpful, but prayer is the only unfailing medication that produces pure happiness.

INSTANT REPLAY

Consider how different our actions would be if instant replay was built into our lives. Every facial expression could be scrutinized, our tone of speech could be reviewed, and our gestures analyzed. We would become more aware of how we present ourselves to the public, and understand why others avoid our companionship.

When my children were younger, I had someone video their birthday parties. As I viewed the films from the parties, I was astounded. I seemed to be frantic in each scene. I constantly cleaned up messes and gave instructions to my daughters, and I hated the person I watched zooming around being controlling. What a rude awakening I experienced! From that point in life, I strove to reign in my frantic behavior. Now, I relax more and clean less. A small amount of disorganization does not leave me distraught. A house that has the "lived-in" look now seems to be more welcoming than it once did.

If the entire human race could review their actions through an instant replay, we would think twice before we spoke or took action. Now we only see the faults in our neighbors, but, with instant replay, we would clearly see ourselves as others see us. With replay, we would learn that our actions are sometimes more detrimental than those of our neighbors whom we criticize.

Indeed, if we learned to scrutinize our intended behavior before we act, a review would not be necessary, and a drastic change would take place in our daily lives. There would be far less need for apologies, and we would understand why our peers dislike being in our company.

In your mind, always remember God IS recording you. Each action IS watched, and every harsh word IS heard. The hateful facial expressions ARE being noted, and one day the world will have access to your deeds. Is that a sobering thought?

BUY NOW, PAY LATER

Today's society is geared toward pleasure now and payment later. Merchandise becomes old and worn before payments are completed. We want instant gratification with no regard for how bills will be paid or how much interest will have accumulated during the wait.

Spiritually we are guilty of the same deed. Whatever sin we are enticed to commit is never weighed in the balances before we act. No thought is given to how or when the payment will be made. We seek pleasure for the moment without considering the penalty our families and loved ones will have to face. When one individual suffers, his loved ones must also bear the burden of the grief or loss. No individual can suffer alone. Always a friend or family member must stand by and watch helplessly as one receives his just dues.

We should always consider the result before purchasing merchandise or making spiritual decisions. There will be less heartache, tears, or broken dreams spent on these purchases and actions, and there will not be the penalty of interest added to our payment. A moment of pleasure is not worth a lifetime of pain.

If our literal diet is considered, we are also seeking instant gratification with our food consumption. Eating whatever we desire as often as we want will also bring delayed payment.

The weight we gain causes our bodies to become unhealthy. A moment of pleasing the taste buds may have to be balanced by hours of exercise and dieting.

Each day one is faced with multiple temptations. If his heart is in tune with God and each desire is tested with thought and prayer, the "buy now, pay later" curse will be eliminated. There will be fewer payments due, less heartache, and a much greater peace of mind. One's stress level will decrease and a lighter heart will abound, since the dreaded due date for payment has been eradicated.

CHRISTIANS ARE GUILTY TOO

What has happened to the days set aside for Christians? We all are guilty of turning God's time into carnal fun and monetary gain.

Easter coincides with spring break for most colleges, and sadly, it is sometimes celebrated with booze and parties. Most parents do not emphasize Christ and His resurrection as the basis of Easter. Rabbits who lay eggs and bring special prizes in baskets to little boys and girls wearing expensive garments and shoes, mar this sacred celebration. No one's mind seems to be centered on the cruel death Jesus suffered and the wondrous resurrection that followed. The youngsters always look forward to hiding eggs and receiving candy, but have they been taught about our Lord?

Thanksgiving has been tarnished with early Christmas displays and rampant shopping. No one even mentions the thankfulness we should feel in our hearts. Food is the only part of Thanksgiving we remember. Should we not consider the safety with which God has blessed our nation, communities, and families? Should we not be on our knees thanking God for our safe passage through life?

The Christmas season has become a time of Santa, gifts, and bright decorations. Some stores and public areas will not allow the mention of Christmas or a replica of a nativity scene to be used. Jesus has been expelled from His own birthday. We receive the parties, gifts, and fun, while He is rejected and made to sit on the outside and weep.

Most children give Santa the honor that Jesus is due. Jesus blessed the parents with the money for the gifts that are attributed to Santa. Little ones believe that Santa has the power to grant their wishes, live-forever, magically fly, and know when they misbehave.

Most of us do not think about the powers that we have given the image that stole Jesus' birthday. We have given Santa the powers that God possesses. What have we become? Should we not be calling our children together and teaching them about the virgin birth of Jesus and the power He has to save their little souls from hell?

I do not know how much pretending God approves of, but I do know the fantasy we have created for our children has overstepped the boundaries.

In addition to these holidays, there is another day God Himself set aside for worship. Most people take Sunday to catch up on whatever was not accomplished during the week. We all claim to rest, even though we shop, clean, play sports, hunt, or fish. Where do we really draw the line? What is the real meaning of Sunday? I know we should use this day for worship and praise, but does all that end when we leave the churchyard? Are we then free to please ourselves?

I am not sure what God would require for these days set aside in His honor. Sunday's expectations He vaguely outlined, but the days man set aside to honor Him have been misused and abused even by man's standards. Since the celebrations have begun to concern me, I feel something is not right. We Christians need to consider if we are helping to bait the very trap that Satan has set. Are we guilty of assisting Satan with his quest to push God right out of our nation?

THE PURE SMILE

An innocent baby has a smile void of deceit. His smile or coo sends joy through the heart of his mom. There is no pretense, just love and contentment. With adults, however, a smile has to be measured and weighed. Was it a friendly smile? Was it a smirk? Was he flirting? Was he making fun? Was he fishing for information by feigning interest?

Very seldom do we see the pure smile of joy and love from an adult. Therefore, the next time you pass someone on the street, go ahead, and smile! This will cause a chain reaction. They too will smile. It is hard to frown into the face of a loving, pleasant smile.

We all hate frowns! However…they too are used to create desired effects.

The next time you pass a mirror, take a peak. Now, that smile you just saw was real. God surely had a since of humor when he made our faces!

PRAYER WORKED BETTER THEN

I was teaching a lesson on Elisha and the Shunammite women (II Kings 4:8-37) to my Sunday school class, and I stressed the power that God had manifested through Elisha when He raised the child from the dead. One young second grade girl raised her hand to speak. Her statement was deep! She said, "Prayer does not work as good now as it did back then." Now, how do you explain that to a child?

I first tried to assure her that God still answers prayers, but that He gave special powers to the prophets of the Old and New Testaments to prove they were the true prophets and were filled with the Spirit of God. The full Bible did not exist during those times, so God added extra proof that He truly was who He proclaimed. They did not have access to the Bible, as we do now. There were only bits and pieces written at that time, and those pieces were not combined for reading.

I am not sure she understood me, but I know I understood her! My mind started churning with thoughts of prayers I had prayed for which I had not received an answer. Am I so weak spiritually that my prayers were not getting higher than the ceiling? Is my faith so weak that God does not honor my request?

There have been times I know God was listening to my plea. His calming presence reassured me that all would be well. He has relieved me of burdens that no one else knew I was carrying, yet there are still unanswered prayers in my life. Why? I truly wish I had the answer. Maybe my timetable and God's are not the same. I read that Abraham was given promises that still have not happened. However, I want my answers now, so maybe part of my problem is lack of patience.

I still ask God for answers to the same prayers I have prayed for years, and I still wonder what is hindering the answer from coming. Just maybe I have found the answer while writing this story. It is just not His will at this time.

THE SHADOW OF HIS HAND

A shadow can be an area of comfort or a cold harsh area of dread. The effects a shadow can have are based upon what is casting the shadow. If it is serving as a block from the sun on a blistering day, then it provides a cool haven. If the shadow is cast from a falling plane, it is an area of horror.

The same scenario applies with the shadows in our lives. Some shadows are places in which one wants always to remain. Some are places in which a person may become comfortable but later learn he has harmed himself by remaining in the shadow too long.

The shadow of God's hand (see Isaiah 51:16) is the most comforting shadow in which one could possibly bask. This is a shadow of restful, peaceful protection, safe from the blistering rays of Satan's power. In God's shadow, a person will never be weathered by the elements of Satan nor scorched by sin.

The longer one stays covered in the shadow of God, the less dominance the pleasures of sin will have over his life. The strain of feeling inferior because of the success of others will become less pervasive in his thoughts. The comfort of knowing one will be protected from Satan's evil force brings a calm assurance that he can face whatever trials the world may send his way.

Are you in the shadow of the cross or in the shadow of sin? Are you living in the shadow of another's success or greatness? Today, step out of any oppressing shadows in your life and exchange them for the shadow of God's loving mercy.

THE DANGER OF SUPRESSED ANGER

When considering anger, an event from several years ago comes to my mind. My family had cleaned the yard of leaves, pine straw, and debris; made a pile; and burned it.

My husband was called away the next week on a work-related trip, so this left my two babies and me at home alone. That day, during the course of eating lunch, one of my daughters claimed she saw smoke in the yard. She had seen correctly!

Although a week had passed, the smoldering embers had remained active. The wind had gotten stronger and had fanned the ashes enough to rekindle the fire. I instantly had trouble on my hands! I commanded the girls to remain inside as I rushed for a water hose to fight the flames.

Buried anger can respond and reappear in much the same way. If hatred is not completely squelched and dealt with, the smoldering embers of resentment will resurface when one is not prepared. There will be neither warning nor anyone on hand to put out the destructive flames.

When dealing with wrath, always get all negative thoughts into the open and deal with them. Conquering feelings of anger and hatred is not only healthy for one's conscience; it is also a great benefit to one's health.

FREE BUT COSTLY

Several years ago, I grew a bumper crop of "ole time petunias" in my flowerbeds. The next growing season hundreds of voluntary plants covered the beds. I called every person in the community who enjoyed planting flowers and welcomed them to free petunias. It was an "all you can take" flower buffet. I felt so smug that my flowers had produced such a great crop of seedlings. These plants proved who really had the green thumb in our community.

Several weeks passed before I realized my petunias were not growing up to look like their ancestors. Something was definitely amiss. These vines began to harden, when petunias are normally very pliable. It took me a moment to realize I had given hundreds of weeds to my friends to plant in their precious flowerbeds! These weeds had fooled everyone who came for the "free" plants. The small sprouts that appeared to be the direct descendants of my "ole time petunias" were impostors. These flower impostors probably hitched a ride to my flowerbeds in the mulch and fertilizer that I had added to the soil.

We should look twice at the free things in life. What costs nothing usually has little value, or, even worse, could be harmful. True gifts usually cost time or money for the giver. Impostor gifts cost the receiver.

Advice is one gift that everyone seems to be quick to hand out. The answer to a problem may seem logical to us, but if God is not leading us to speak, we need to remain silent. All advice should be sown in prayer, fertilized with the Word, and watered with tears.

If, when you are tempted to give advice, you follow this growth process, you will know what God wants you to say. Even though the gift of silence is very hard to give, there are times He wants you to say nothing.

TAPROOT

A taproot is a primary root that forms first and grows directly from the plant stem. It grows thicker than the other roots and stores food for the rest of the plant. This describes the nourishing structure of some plants, but it could describe the moral structure of a growing child.

With a weak taproot, a plant will have less chance of surviving the challenges of low moisture and poor soil. If a healthy taproot is in place, stored nutrients will be available and readily supplied to the plant when needed. The storage of nutrients takes place as the taproot grows to support the plant, not when the plant experiences need.

The basic structure or foundation of a child needs to be strong enough to supply the child with moral and spiritual nourishment even when the surrounding world has poor nutrients available. If the child's taproot is not strong and growing in the rich soil of love and moral teachings, there is a greater chance of a weak, wilting, spiritually dry individual who struggles to survive the winds of life.

The key to the taproot is its growth, unseen to the naked eye, in the darkness below the ground's surface. No one can look at a young plant and know if a healthy taproot has been formed. That will become obvious when difficult growing conditions occur. By the time structural problems present themselves, it will be almost impossible to administer enough nourishment to save the fading plant.

During a child's carefree youth, the nourishments for a strong, spiritual individual should be absorbed into his inner core. The daily conversations a child encounters help to mold his thought patterns and cause his mind's roots to grow deep in his preference for worldly sin or the love of God. The amount of time a child spends watching television or listening to secular music should be monitored. Parents need to know what information is being fed into their children's tender minds, because they will be responsible for the formation of their little taproots. Parents are not always available when problems arise and their children are faced with choices that will permanently alter the course of their lives, but the nutrition parents helped to store inside the children's hearts will then guide their decisions.

I shudder to think how healthy my children's taproots would be if I had been the only influence in their growing and maturing years. Grandparents, family members, friends, and neighbors played an important role in the nourishment given to my children. The extra guidance and tender warnings they offered to my daughters helped to make them who they are today.

PRACTICE MAKES PERFECT

Making the right choices in life is a constant process, so let us start practicing today! Webster defines practice as "to perform or work at repeatedly so as to become proficient." There is no better time than now to start practicing.

One person can make a difference. Starting today, let this one be YOU! Whom could you befriend? Do you know someone struggling with his studies? Is someone showing signs of pressure from home? If you know anyone who seems in need, you are the person to stand up to the task and show love. A kind word, a pat on the back, or a big smile could be all it takes to unlock the gates that are obstructing his happiness.

Could one person have made a difference in our history? One thinks of coos, smiles, giggles, and unadulterated love when babies are mentioned, but, just remember, Hitler was once a baby. What went wrong? Were the love, kindness, and teaching not given to him? Could one loving person have changed the course of his life? If love had been shown to him, would the world's history books be without a world war that he ignited? Would thousands of Jews still be living to raise their children?

You may never befriend a world leader, but every person you meet is just as important, because he is a soul bound for heaven or hell. Your friendship could change the course of his life and cause others to be safe from his possible future criminal acts, so start practicing today.

CATCHING WAVES

How many different signals are surrounding us at this very moment? Radio, television, cell phone, short wave, computer, and who knows what other waves are zooming around us. The amazing part is that we cannot see or hear them unless we have the correct instrument or "ear" to receive them. Even changing the channel on these instruments determines which waves are received.

Could the spiritual ear of our heart be blocked from receiving God's message due to an inadequate receiver? Are we broken or on the wrong channel for God's waves to penetrate? Could our "out of tune life" filter out the spiritual signals God is transmitting?

There could be several reasons our prayer waves are short-circuited. We can stray from the fold of God and wander in the world's wilderness beyond the reach of spiritual signals. The devil's messages can bleed through on our static-filled line with God, and the world can run an interference block in our heart's receivers.

Some nights I use a headset to listen to the television. This allows me to relax while watching and not disturb my husband's sleep. There have been occasions when I walked out of the range of the television signals reaching my headset. A distant sound of diverse radio programs could be heard as

I moved around, but as soon as I returned to the range of my headset transmitter, I could again hear the television.

Sometimes it does not take very many steps in the wrong direction to leave the boundaries of God's heart signals. We think the few wrongs we commit could not hinder our prayers, but we should think again. God expects us to live with a prayerful heart, meaning to keep a continual prayer line open and in use. If this prayer line is up and running, there will be instant access to God's throne when problems arise.

OUR SPIRITUAL MAKEUP

Most women practice a routine of beautifying themselves before going into public. The person who looked in the morning mirror looks nothing like the person who leaves the house to face the day. We, as women, pride ourselves in presenting the best face we can to the public. Our rumpled hair, nondescript eyes, dull skin, and unjeweled ears and neck are all adorned to perfection before the grand exit from home.

We would not dream of allowing a picture of our real appearance to be publicly displayed. The only image we want others to associate us with is the polished, staged look we have taken great pains to create. Our real appearance is enhanced with makeup, hair styling, and jewelry, thus creating a faux impression.

People are also guilty of producing faux impressions with their Christian lives. The stage makeup they apply before going into church or a Christian crowd is much the same as women practice with their appearance. The public has no knowledge of what the everyday lives of most Christians are. The places they go, manner of speech they use, and actions they display determine their true character, not the brief display seen in spiritual company. When they are facing those they want to impress, a hypocritical smile can easily replace the smirks used in daily life.

Does the world see a different character from that you show during Sunday morning services? Do your fellow workers hear you speak words you would never dream of using in a crowd of Christians? Do you attend places where you would not want to see a fellow church member? Do you fear someone's seeing you in your natural habitat when no spiritual makeup has been applied?

I am sure every person in this world has moments of regret. No one would want every moment of his life exposed, but remember there is a record being made of our lives that will be exposed to the entire world. God does not only record our "makeup" moments; He has a thorough record of all the moments of our life.

PLACING BLAME

Exhausted, I retired to bed early and left my husband to continue a visit with his company on our porch. After the visitor left, my husband came inside, and he too retired for the night. My guess is that he did not come in alone, because during the night, I awoke with the uneasy feeling that something had touched my arm. Still half asleep, I felt something move from my shoulder to my face. With one giant swoop of my hand, I grabbed the largest bug I have ever seen and slung it to the floor, turned on the light, and squashed the bug with a shoe. My thoughts raced as to how a bug that large could get inside. It must have hitched a ride on my husband's clothing. Anything that large had to have the door held open for it to enter. So, for a moment I lay there and blamed him for the episode.

The next morning my first words to him were, "Do you know what you did last night?"

His answer was a simple statement that he was innocently asleep and got the blame for something he knew nothing about.

Later it came to me how we always blame someone for the unfortunate things that happen to us. It is much easier to place blame on someone else than to accept our own faults. Our first impulse is to figure out who might have caused the circumstance in which we have found ourselves. It could never be totally our fault, because fault loves company. Someone had to assist.

I still have not apologized to him. I still think he brought the bug inside and it should have crawled onto HIS face! One thing is for sure; I did not hear it ring the doorbell, and I did not welcome it in, so I know I am innocent.

LIFE'S ROAD MAP

When we start a road trip, we purchase a road map of the area from our home base to wherever we plan to travel. If the route and distance are calculated, time and money can be saved. Before we begin the journey, we need a general idea of the path we need to travel, the approximate number of gas refills, the number of motels needed, the price of sites we will explore, and the time involved to complete the trip. With this information, we are able to determine how much money we will need. When all the details are planned, we then feel confident and prepared for travel.

Looking down at a road map is somewhat like looking through the pages of the Bible. With each, we see the beginning and the ending destination of our journey. We also see many different side roads that if chosen will either enhance or deter our journey. A map can direct us to any place we desire to go. It is up to us to follow the path marked and not deviate onto the wrong exit. The Bible has directions to heaven and hell, and it is up to us to follow the heavenly direction. If the devil can fill our minds with the struggles of life and hinder us from turning to God, he can cause us to travel the road to hell. Simply believing in Jesus seems too simple for our mortal minds. We want to strive or work our way to Him when all He has commanded is for us to believe.

That seems much too easy, so we exit off into works, detour into sacrifice, or yield toward attaining perfection.

Even our Christian lives seem filled with worldly pleasures that beckon and cause us to deviate from the course that God has mapped. If we had the vision to see what our wayward exits would cost in the end, we would then have more determination to ignore the worldly enticements. We read where God's promises are made to the enduring Christian, but we still have problems keeping our vision on the straight and narrow road. If we Christians struggle with the wooing of the world, how much harder is it for someone who has no relationship with God? Satan is second in power to God, and he uses this power to confuse the believer and blind the unbeliever.

On a map, we can trace a road and know where it leads. In life, we choose a path and depend on God to direct our steps. If we have started in the wrong direction, God has the ability to reveal to us where our missteps are leading. Christians sometimes travel toward personal or financial success only to reach a dead end. God has a purpose for every detour, dead end, and stop sign He erects in our paths. If we keep a close relationship with Him, he will guide our travels and reward us at the end of the journey. If we refuse to allow God to guide, our exit from this life will lead to a sorrowful loss of rewards in heaven.

When I read the journey of the children of Israel, I wonder how they could have been so disgruntled and disobedient. God had promised them the Canaan land, but their doubts cost the lives of all but two of the original adults that left Egypt. Out of thousands that were issued a promise by God, only two enjoyed the fruits of the forty-year journey and settled in Canaan. Why did they not believe, and why did they doubt that God would deliver them? We are just like them. They could not see the ending of the map God had laid out for them. They had to believe that He would do exactly what He said even when times seemed so severe and all seemed lost. We see how He always came through and fed, watered, and protected them, but they were looking from the other end of the road. Believing something will happen is much more difficult than believing something did happen.

In the book of Genesis, Joseph stayed true to God through persecution by his brothers, lies by Potiphar's wife, and time in prison. He had no idea that being true to God would one day lead to his being ruler over the land of Egypt. He maintained a close walk with God through the dark days of his youth even though every day presented a new trial. We see where it paid him to serve God, but he did not know where his path was leading during those dark, lonesome hours. He lived believing that serving God was more important than having approval of man.

The three Hebrew children were cast into fire for not bowing to an idol. They knew God was able to deliver them, but He had not promised them He would. They were traveling their path believing it would pay to follow God's will even if it took their lives.

Daniel was cast into the den of lions for praying. God did not promise Daniel deliverance even though He did close the lions' mouths and protected him. Looking back, we think he knew how it all would end, but he did not. He walked his path in faith and believed God would treat him right.

We too have promises that will be granted if we walk with God, but Satan has the power to turn our heads and cause doubts whenever we pause in our journey and look to the world. We must look toward the end of our journey knowing we will not be mistreated. We may not accomplish what we want, but we will accomplish what God has called us to do.

If at your death a map could be made of the roads you traveled through life, would you want your children to follow it? Would the paths you took be a spiritual guide map or a worldly guide map for those behind to follow? Will God reward you for your life's path, or will you hang your head in shame when you meet Him? On the other hand, have you ignored the map God gave for heaven and followed Satan to destruction? If so, you surely would not want your children to follow your example. Since most children follow the lead of their parents, should you not study the road you are traveling? Make sure it leads to heaven and is following the path that God planned for your life.

JUST A DROP OF WATER

If I could be as useful in the Lord's service as just a single drop of water is to this earth, oh what a difference I could make! Multitudes of lives could be touched, numerous heartaches could be mended, and the soul's thirst could be quenched. One drop seems so small, but its ability to be transformed into liquid, solid, or gas could set an example to us of the flexible nature by which we need to adhere to God's service.

A drop in God's service could wash away hurt, moisten the lips and throat for speaking, caress a sad face, wash a wound, or cool a fevered brow of sin. A raindrop of nature can water soil for plant growth, descend from a beautiful waterfall, stop fires, bear ships upon the sea, cool a drink, preserve our food, or moisten a parched tongue.

I pray that I can be used in God's service in whatever form He chooses for me and stay as flexible as a single drop of water. Wherever He chooses me to go and in which form He desires for me to portray Him, let me always be willing to wash the fevered brow or to help bear the weight of a massive ship.

PERSONAL APPEARANCE

Saying it is hard for me to buy clothes off the rack is really an understatement! My height hinders me from purchasing very many items this way. Nothing is long enough, and when I try on new clothes, I feel like an amazon in short britches.

Lack of clothing that fits me correctly was weighing heavily on my mind while I was ironing last Saturday night. My daughter entered the room sporting a new outfit. I admired the clothes she had purchased that day and commented that I needed her to shop for me, since I was tired of looking like a hag. Her reply took me by surprise. She responded that new clothes would not change that!

Now this child is always witty, so I showed mock shock and pretended to tattle to her dad. His reply did shock me! He stated that clothing would not help my looks; it could only enhance my appearance. Hm, you know, he might really be on to something, but do not tell him I said so. I had never thought about it like that.

The same statement could apply to Christians. We can look the part, but just the outward appearance being altered will not clean our hearts and lives before God. The world may be fooled into thinking we are striving to follow the Spirit, but we can never fool God. He looks on the inward man. Our

Sunday attire and our saintly actions at God's house do not fool Him. He hears the words that proceed from our mouth during daily activities and knows the thoughts of our heart wherever we are.

I have not gotten new clothes, but maybe I can let my adornment be a smile and a kind word instead of expensive attire. New clothes could have built up my confidence, but a kind word may build up my neighbor's confidence.

SHE DID WHAT I SAID

My daughters had visited a little friend for a day of play. That afternoon I noticed welts across my younger daughter's legs. I asked her what had happened to cause those streaks! She stated they had been playing house, and she was the other girl's baby. The girl had pretended she had been bad and gave her a whipping with a switch. When I heard that, I nearly came unglued at the seams!!!

We sat down and had a major talk. She informed me I had told her not to fight and to be sweet, so she had to take the whipping. I informed her she DID NOT have to take the whipping. I told her the next time that happened for her to say, "My Mother said for me to knock you down."

A few days rocked by and I had forgotten the encounter. My daughters again were invited to play, so I drove over to drop them off. When my baby daughter stepped out of the car, she announced in the loudest voice she could muster, "My Mother said for me to knock you down today!"

I nearly died!

Through anger, I had given her instructions that she did not fully understand. I realized I had taught them to be too submissive when I had stressed for them to be nice, but I had truly gone astray by trying to over compensate for my failure in not teaching her to take up for herself. Boy, can't parents make a mess!

Do you sometimes wish God had given us an entire book on rearing children? I know I do. I have made all the mistakes possible. Sometimes I wonder how my children turned out to be as good as they are. I have truly been blessed.

FAITH OF A CHILD

When my baby daughter was around three years of age, she decided to pack her suitcase and run away. She came into the kitchen lugging her little pink case filled with whatever she thought was important. She announced she was running away and that Marc, my nephew, was coming to get her. I asked her how she knew he would come. She said she just knew! I went to the back phone, called him, and relayed the story. When I returned to the kitchen, I realized she had gone outside to wait for him without saying anything more to me.

Of course, I ran out and took pictures as she crawled into his car and waved "bye" to me. I waited for some time and then drove over to Marc's and picked her up. I asked her why Marc came to our house. She told me he knew she wanted to run away, so he came to get her. It never crossed her mind that I had instigated his coming. She had blind faith. If Marc loved her as much as she loved him, she felt that he automatically knew she wanted to run away!

Several days later she got a bar stool, placed it under the wall phone in the kitchen, and proceeded to sit and sit and sit. I asked her why she was sitting there and she answered that Michael, another nephew, was calling her. "Why do you think he is calling?" I asked.

"Because I want him to," was her reply.

Once again I intervened by calling from the back phone. Later, when the phone rang she said, "I told you he'd call!"

She picked up the receiver and said, "Hi Michael!" with no doubt that he would be on the line.

We have been given promises that God would take care of our needs, but I still have doubts whenever problems arise. If I could only have the faith of a child, my life would be less stressful. God does know what we are thinking; "Just because He loves us." I never turn my cares over to Him until I have worn them out dragging them back and forth to His throne. Giving up and believing He will do what He promised is easier said than done!

NO RETURNS

When I was homeschooling my daughters, we had many hours of communicating. Some of these talking sessions turned into preaching sessions (so the girls claimed). On one such occasion, I was explaining to them that I had not reared children before they came along, and I was sure I would make mistakes. I stressed that if they thought I had treated them unfairly or disciplined them too harshly, they should talk with me at a time when we were able to discuss the issue in calm terms. If I felt I had been too hard on them, I would apologize. I explained that I was still learning and would make mistakes.

My younger daughter was about six at the time and did not fully understand why her mom would not know everything. After a moment of thought she stated, "We did not come with a receipt, so you can't take us back!" I laughingly explained to her that just because I was inexperienced and made mistakes did not mean I was incapable of rearing them.

Being mistreated through a mistake is not a problem we have with our Heavenly Father. He never has a need to apologize to His children. We can always rest assured that the treatment we receive is a lighter sentence than we truly deserve. There will never be a chance that He will return us no matter what sins we commit. His purchase is forever and continues beyond death.

If we could have the wisdom of God when we correct our children, we could rear a generation of loving and trusting individuals that could change the world one child at a time.

INSTRUCTIONS IN ADVANCE

I received a call to fill in for an absent teacher at the local school. Upon reaching my classroom for the day, I found the door locked. Later, I located a teacher from down the hall who had access to the key I needed. Lying on the desk inside the classroom was a neat note with instructions for me. The note stated, "Ask Mrs. Jones to unlock my door for you. Be sure she knows to lock it again in the afternoon after you leave." There were my instructions! I had received them, but it was after the critical moment of need had passed. This was not a major incident, just comical.

I filed this experience away to later use as an instructional story. I am always seeing important lessons in little moments we experience in our daily activities. I wondered how many times we give instructions to our youth after they have already faced the problem or temptation of which we are warning them.

Never say, "It will not happen to my child!" This statement provides a red flag in the face of the devil; he will use your denial as a catalyst for his evil. It CAN happen to your child. One misguided acquaintance could influence your child to misbehave and turn his back on the teachings you have tried to instill in him. A child will do far more when accompanied by someone who feeds and pressures him with twisted misinformation than he would ever think to do alone.

Empower your child with different scenarios he may face. Explain that there are actions he may take to remove himself from temptation. Warn him to question any suggestions that are contrary to what he has been taught. ALWAYS assure him that you will be there for support if he makes a bad choice and you will come to his rescue no matter what time of day or night he may call you. Assure him that he will be picked up and carried home without being harassed or receiving punishment until both of you have had a chance to consider the event. At this time serious discussion will be needed and due punishment will be considered.

Make sure your children know they will be loved no matter what evil they may commit. You do not love the disobedient deed, but you will always love the child even though he disobeys.

IF ALL WERE LOST

Most people look at their homes, cars, clothing, and material wealth and feel that they have so little, when really they are rich and unaware of their blessings. A person only learns truly to appreciate his belongings after they have been taken away. A companion never fully understands the love he feels for his mate until she is gone. A woman never considers her youthful looks as beautiful until age has bathed her with mature features; she may then realize what youthful beauty she possessed.

If through some fluke of nature one could have all his earthly possessions removed for a short period and then have them restored, he would realize the great wealth he possesses. Consider if one lost his home, car, clothing, photographs, and money in one instant. Now, consider if all could be returned to him after his grieving and counting the loss. Receiving the same goods again would make him feel rich, blessed, and satiated! One does not fully appreciate his gifts and treasures until he no longer possesses them.

PERSISTECE PAYS

Since I was the only school teacher my children would have from kindergarten through grade twelve, I took every opportunity I could to teach them what could lie ahead in their lives. My daughters called it sermons, but I called it teaching. I felt they were somewhat living in a cocoon. We had a vast number of family and friends with whom we intermingled daily, but the lessons learned from school activities and acceptance trials would not be theirs to have.

One afternoon while my daughters and I were sitting on the front porch talking, I noticed a few sprigs of grass had pushed their way through the gravel bed of our circle drive. We had planted grass seeds over our front lawn since we had installed the new circle drive and leveled the front yard with the tractor blade. All that was left of our lawn was a seeded dirt bed. Continuous watering with sprinklers over the soft soil had not produced much grass cover over the past few weeks. With all the care given to the lawn, the grass was stubbornly refusing to appear, but where no disking, fertilizing, or watering had taken place stood a healthy patch of grass in the middle of a roadbed!

I told my daughters to study the yard for a moment and tell me what they thought of the grass. Had it been given every opportunity to thrive? Had we nourished the seeds and soil with fertilizer and water? They agreed that we had done our best. I mentioned the grass in the road. Had we given it the same opportunity as the lawn? Of course, we had not. Now we compared the height and size of the blades. The gravel grass won easily.

Next, our discussion turned to my daughters. I explained that Clay and I had tried to give them every opportunity to grow and thrive in life. What they did with these opportunities was strictly their decision. They could thrive and become useful Christians who made an honest living or they could become people who had no desire to better themselves. I explained that some children seemed to have everything working against them but still managed to persevere and achieve much in life. These people had to dig deep for the water and fertilizer needed to grow into adulthood, thus making them more solid, strong, and deep. When one strives through hardships to attain a goal, he appreciates the victory more than the person who was been given everything needed to form a solid foundation on which to build.

The choice to persist or give up is before every person in this world. Are you going to rise to the occasion and better yourself even if you were not privileged to be nurtured? Will you be the grass growing, against all odds, in the tightly packed gravel of a driveway or the person who has been blessed to receive every opportunity possible and not accomplish your potential? I am truly afraid I am the grass in the yard. That is why I want my children to strive to be as tough as gravel grass!

NOAH'S PROMISE

How many times would you encourage someone to turn from wrong? Would you continue to plead with them for 100 years? According to the Bible, Noah preached about 100 years to the lost world and pled with the people until God closed the door of the ark. The Bible states in II Peter 4:5 that he was a preacher of righteousness. Seemingly, no one paid his messages any attention since his family were the only ones saved from the flood. God promised Noah that He would protect his family if he followed His instructions and built an ark. Noah did his part; God protected his family.

This all seems like a fairy tale, since we have heard this story since birth, but there really was a man named Noah who built an ark. He was different from every other person in his world. He listened to God while others scoffed at the big boat he was building on dry land. There had never been rain on this earth at that time. God had watered the soil with a mist that came from the ground, so when Noah mentioned a flood, his words seemed foreign. We tend to seek approval from our fellow man, but Noah did not. He followed God and continued to spread the warning.

God closed the door of the ark (Genesis 17:16). This was a sign that He was pleased with a job well done. The people outside the ark would have no more chances to turn to God and escape the flood. When the water drops started to fall, I am sure several people started to question their decisions to mark Noah off as crazy. They had never seen water falling, heard thunder roll, or experienced any type of storm. Their thoughts probably turned to the man who had preached for years and was now safe inside the ark. Just maybe he did teach the truth after all.

In my mind, I can see crowds racing to the ark, knocking on the walls, and begging Noah to let them enter. They could not get inside since God closed the door. If it had been left to Noah, he surely would have saved everyone who begged to come aboard, but it was not his decision. A door closed by God cannot be opened by man.

Did Noah enjoy the moment when the clouds released their water and God proved he had been right? I think not. He knew the people had not really rejected him; they had rejected God. He also knew he would never see any faces from his past again. Everything that would later live and breathe on land was loaded on the very ark he had built. No other person or land creature would survive.

If someone seems not to pay attention to my conversation, I find another person more attentive with whom to talk. Never would I plead with them for years to listen to me.

If no one on earth approved of my vocation except my companion and children, I would seriously consider changing. Most everyone wants public approval.

If all I could do for months was feed animals and visit with the same few family members in a confined space with no change of scenery, I would become dissatisfied and cantankerous. There is no record of family problems on board the ark.

Since most people hate ridicule, crave public approval, and enjoy diverse company, whom would God choose today if he needed an ark? Could He depend on us? Would we quit after the first week of public humiliation? Would we build from the blueprint or find a better way? Would we be so out of sorts with God that we would not even finish the project? Can He truly depend on us?

There is still a message to carry. The Lord is coming back and claiming His own. Are all our friends and family ready? Is there someone on the road to hell to whom we can talk? Are we being called to do a service for God but are too ashamed to be different?

GENTLE REMINDERS

No child is perfect, but everyone thinks his is close! I was blessed with humble, obedient children, but there were times they had to have a little reminder to straighten things out. One chore they never seemed to remember in their youth was making up their bed. I tired telling, scolding.... but nothing seemed to jog their memory. One morning they had gone upstairs to the schoolroom, and, again, I found their bed in disarray. Now what could I do to help them remember? I wrote them a note stating how I had lovingly covered their cold bodies with my skirts, provided them with a place to rest their weary heads and protection during the long nights. I asked them if they could please do one favor for me. Could they please remember to cover my nakedness that they had been leaving exposed every day? Could they treat me with the respect that I had given to them? Could they please spread my garment skirts across my body each morning before leaving the room? I signed the note with "your bed."

Neither child said a word after she found the note. Instead of my scolding, there was a kind letter asking for their help. It worked! For days, I never had to ask them to make their bed.

Do we try God's patience? I know He has given me gentle reminders many times. If I do not seem to understand the gentle reminders, then He gives me a bump in the road. If I do not turn around for the bump, then comes a hard strike of understanding. The strike of God's hand a person will not soon forget. Instead of a moment of tears, He can generate a flood of tears that will last for what seems an endless period. His patience is more enduring than a parent's patience, but where parents tend not to be consistent in what is right or wrong, God never changes His mind. If He says *no*, then the answer will be *no*.

I pray that I can recognize the gentle reminders in life and adhere to God's will. I dislike the bumps in the road, but I fear the strikes.

HOT TOPIC

At the local deli, I purchased meat that had been rolled in spices. My older daughter (about thirteen at the time) decided to taste test the meat. A few bites later, she was wailing in pain! A large flake of hot pepper had lodged between her front tooth and gums. I did everything I could to remove the flake, but it would not budge. Since we live only five miles from our country dentist, down the road we sped for help. He had the flake removed within seconds and stated I would never have reached it without a dental tool. What seemed so minor on the surface had caused severe pain.

One night I could not rest, so I spent time reminiscing about my daughters' childhood antics. This particular episode replayed itself in my mind. At first, I chuckled about what my girls always seemed to get into, but then I saw the symbolism of comparing the pepper to sin.

A small speck of sin can cause great pain in our lives until it has been removed. The removal may not be an easy task. The right tools are necessary to reach the problem. Just saying, "Sorry Lord, but you know I'm human," will not bring results. For the prayer to produce results, a sorrowful heart must be honest and open with God before seeking forgiveness. God expects us to remove ourselves from the offending situation and leave it behind us. Returning to the same weakness is not acceptable, so we must be continually in prayer for our weaknesses.

It is so great that we have a forgiving God who hears our sincere prayers. I have returned to His throne many times seeking His forgiveness, and as I write this story I am searching my life, checking for flakes of sin that are lodged out of sight that could be hindering my service for Him. I do not want to wait until the sin starts burning a hole in my conscience!

FAITH SHAKEN

We never taught our children to believe in Santa, the Easter Bunny, or the Tooth Fairy. We always joked with them about these characters, but we made sure they understood who actually supplied the goodies.

One Easter weekend my husband Clay was to have back surgery; therefore, we would not be able to be with our daughters on Easter Sunday. We decided to present them with their baskets before we left for the hospital. The night before he entered the hospital, Clay went outside and placed their Easter baskets on the front porch mat, rang the doorbell, and re-entered the house through the back door. The girls opened the front door as Clay reached the entrance to the living room. The screaming that followed was unreal! They thought the Easter Bunny must really exist! On the porch mat was the proof of his existence! We talked for quite a while before convincing them that Clay had actually made a trip around the house before they had opened the door. Even though my daughters had been taught that the Bunny was just an imaginary character, their faith in our word had been deeply shaken.

Our Christian faith can be shaken just this easily. What we think we strongly believe can be shaken by the devil when we are least expecting it. We believe we have great faith, until the devil decides to throw a roadblock in our path and shake our faith in God. How close we are to God at the time of a trial will determine how much power the devil will have over us.

The devil, who is second in power to God, knows exactly when to put us to the test. He usually waits until we are rocking along smoothly and have let down our guard. He knows we are less likely to veer from our beliefs while having a close walk with the Master, so he chooses times of contentment with no major problems that would have encouraged us to lean heavily upon God. When the going gets easy, the perfect door of opportunity squeaks open, and the devil can take full advantage of our resting our armor of defense.

EXTREME WEATHER SIGNS

When I was a child, my grandfather showed me a smeared rainbow in the sky. He explained it as an extreme weather sign that warned of unusual rain, drought, or storms soon to come. I never had the privilege of seeing many more of these signs until recently.

Walking through the parking lot after a day of shopping, I saw an old pickup truck with a reflecting back glass. There in the reflection was a beautiful extreme weather sign! I looked up toward the clouds and searched for the sign; there was not one but two smeared rainbows high in the clouds. No one else seemed to be impressed by these. I stood there for some time and clicked pictures of the beautiful sight.

I started toward home still snapping photos through the windshield of my van. I called my two daughters and husband, who were all in different places, and told them to go outside and look. None of them could see the signs. I made a stop at the local pharmacy and removed my shades before entering the building, and, guess what, the smeared rainbows almost vanished when I removed the tinted glass from my eyes. I slipped them on and off in amazement at the difference the lenses made when shielding the glare. The nonexistent rainbows snapped back into place each time I returned the shades to my eyes. It seemed that this beautiful sight was meant for me alone.

The pictures I took during this beautiful display were mostly just glare and clouds. A small glimmer of smeared colors was visible after I enlarged and enhanced the photos. This was the only proof I had to show that I had not lost my mind. After raving on and on over the beauty of the colors, I had nothing but specks on a photo for proof.

Could this be the view a Christian has in comparison to the world's view? God gives us a Spiritual vision that the nonbeliever does not possess. Without the guidance of God, so much beauty is lost. The warning signs go unnoticed because of carnal blindness.

Since Spiritual vision cannot be purchased and can only be received through becoming God's child, we should be announcing to the world the grave need to repent and become focused on God.

LEARNING TO FLY

A bird built her nest in our front porch fern. She worked diligently, carrying each twig and placing it inside the hanging plant so that the wind would not disturb her future young. For days, she built the nest, sat on the eggs, protected the new babies, and provided entertainment for our family.

We rooted for the babies as each day we watched their little heads, with mouths thrown open, pop over the fern, waiting for their mother's anticipated feeding. Out of curiosity, we tilted the fern and peeked into the nest to see the size of the young. Each tilt caused the little babies to throw their mouths open.

The day finally arrived when the babies were precariously perched on the nest's edge to view the outside world. They were given lessons on flying. The parents sat on our porch rail and the surrounding flowerbed borders and flapped their wings. I was touched by these portrayals of teaching and love.

Once the test flight came, the danger began. The first bird left the nest and bounced in the grass below. Within seconds danger appeared in the form of dogs. Our two black Labs instantly darted over and captured the innocent bird. My screaming and grabbing did not help. The bird lay dead beside the large dog, and my heart sank. My first thought was that this is just like the devil. Parents do all they can to protect and teach, but the devil is always waiting in some form to destroy whomever he can capture. He does not care how hard parents have worked to teach their youth the truth, how hard they struggled to give their children the best, how innocent and beautiful the children may be, or how sad the parents will be when the damage is done.

As soon as our children leave our doorway and step into the world, the devil has an open gate to enter their lives. He does not discriminate. Everyone is his target. His nature, just like that of the dogs, is to destroy and dominate our children. We should always be in much prayer each time our children step into this wicked world. The devil is lurking just beyond the ferns that hang from our front porch.

A SNAKE IN THE NEST

Birds do not seem to learn from their mistakes. A second bird nest was started in the same hanging, porch fern mentioned in "Learning to Fly." I tried to deter the bird from making the same mistake twice. I tore down what she had built, but she just started over. My next roadblock was to place a rubber snake across the nest with the head turned upward. After a series of dive bombing trips toward the snake, she realized there was no harm in this one. She continued to build the nest around the offending object!

Of course, this gave me food for thought. The snake could symbolize the devil in our lives. When he appears and tries to block the success we are making or our growth in the Lord, we usually get discouraged and back away from our original plans. It does not take much discouragement to stop the Lord's work in our lives. Instead of depending on the Lord for guidance and strength, we pull away and claim the path is too hard to travel.

The bird realized the nest was important, because she had to have a home built for her future young. The eggs could not wait for her to draw up another plan of action. She depended on her instincts to determine if there was real danger or if someone was just stalling her progress.

How much time have we lost starting and stopping in our service for God? When the way seems tough, we tend to hunt an easier way. When the road gets long and we retreat, we may never realize that the devil has just won a major battle in our lives. If he can continue to throw up a roadblock at every important turn in the building process of our spiritual lives, he can mastermind our future without our ever recognizing his tactics.

CREDIT WHERE CREDIT IS DUE

Have you ever watched the film credits roll at the ending of a film? If you had participated in the production, would you be watching intently for your name? Sure, you would. You would notify all your friends so they too could watch for your acknowledgments. However, if the film were a miserable failure, would you still be anxious to acknowledge your part?

The nature of humankind causes us to want all to acknowledge our achievements and to announce to the world any measure of success. However, the opposite is true of failures. We tell all those we can about our successes, but never discuss our failures.

If I were an influence in the life of someone who gained wealth, greatness, fame, prestige, or other accolades, I would feel honored to have my name intimately linked with theirs. I might even feel this person was entitled to a public honorary mention.

If I were an influence in the life of someone who went dreadfully astray, would I still want the credit? Would I want my name listed as a producer in his failures? If my harsh judgments, gossip, or example led him astray, would I still want my name linked with his?

The successful influences we crave to announce. The failures to which we have contributed are an embarrassment from which we strive to distance ourselves. Both may have been productions in which we participated, but we only want the public to know the positive. The private moments we use to gossip and destroy are the same moments we want hidden from the world. The disaster we may have helped to produce is no longer a subject of our gossip. We distance ourselves from any mention of the failure, afraid the part we played will be discovered.

Should the credits be listed on my life, I wonder if my name would be listed with more failures than successes? Have I been a person intent on gossiping and hurting others or encouraging and building others' confidence? We may be responsible for more harm than we realize. Our careless words or actions may have driven some to their downfall.

The next time I take credit for something wonderful I have done, I need to be careful not to be over confident about my contribution. There could be several people waiting in the wings to give me credit for their failures.

NEVER SATISFIED

I have always been blessed with a good automobile, but I have never owned a new one. Money always seemed too tight to satisfy some selfish desire when things that are more important were needed. A car was a car and that was all, until one year when I saw the new Lincoln. Now that was a car! Why I wanted one is beyond me, but, at the time, it seemed important. I never asked for one because I knew that would be a foolish investment, and, besides, I had a perfectly good car. A new car would lose value when its tires left the parking lot at the dealership. It would be considered a used product and be worth much less than the "new car."

My husband did not understand my fascination with this car. One morning we got into my "trusty" car to make the trip to church. Clay looked at me and asked, "Now look, this car has everything on it that the Lincoln has. Why don't you like this car just the same?"

I responded with, "I have everything that God gave Marilyn Monroe. There is just something about the arrangement that makes the difference."

No, I did not get the car; I just learned to be satisfied with what I had. Are we not all the same in some way? We want what others have - such as talent, fame, luxury, prestige, wealth, beauty - when we have been given exactly what we need.

After God made us to His liking and gave us what He wanted us to have, we still are not satisfied. There are moments I realize how blessed I have been and apologize for all the petty problems I think I am facing. I may not look as nice, be as wealthy, drive new cars, or have fame, but God loves me just as I am. He does not want to rearrange His plan to fit my desires for things of no value.

IF WE NEVER MEET AGAIN

My day started earlier than usual. I had much on my agenda and too few hours to complete the errands. I packed my van and started down the drive. My eyes caught sight of a white object in the yard. I drove closer to see if it was a baseball that had been left outside; no, it was just a giant mushroom that had sprung up overnight. Instantly, I thought about what a great story that mushroom would make. It represented some people's religion. They are all fired up for the Lord but do not study and put down roots. The first problem that comes along knocks them over and destroys their faith.

While driving further down the drive, I was praying aloud about a burden that I had been carrying for quite some time. I asked God if He would please give me guidance as to whether or not He wanted me to publish my stories to the public in book form or just keep them for my family. I opened the mailbox, and there was only one envelope inside. It was addressed to me. A publishing company was answering my e-mail. Yes, they would publish my book! I instantly called my husband and told him I had my answer. I felt God had made it perfectly clear what He wanted me to do.

The letter stated that within 90 days my book could be completed. That is only three months! Was my dream coming to fruition? Was I sure I wanted others to read my private thoughts?

In town, I visited Wal-Mart for mission shoebox supplies. Several church members had given me money to purchase these supplies. This was not my money I was spending, so I took it very seriously. I stood at the rack of clearance items and asked God for guidance in making my selections. I gathered up several items and asked a sales clerk if she knew where their best clearance deals were located. She went to her supervisor and received permission for me to select as many clearance shirts as needed, and they would only cost $1.00 each! I left with eighty shirts plus a stack of socks and toys. God multiplied the spending power of that money!

I was having a perfect day! I drove from store to store singing and thanking God for answering my prayers. My last stop for the day was for hair supplies at a local beauty supply store. I parked next to the end curb and exited my van. My foot caught on the curb and rolled my left ankle. I caught on my hands just before kissing the pavement. Much to my dismay, an eighteen-wheeler was parked about 12 feet in front of me, being unloaded by several burly men. They never missed a beat unloading the clothes racks of tuxedos, but I knew I had just made a public spectacle of myself. I was humiliated but, most of all, I was in pain.

My first thoughts were, "Why did this have to happen and ruin such a perfect day... I can't walk... but I'm sure not going to crawl.... Oh, just get a grip and walk... OH, I can't... But I have to."

I finally gritted my teeth and walked with as much dignity as I could muster. I entered the beauty supply shop and was met with a smile and a "May I help you?" Now, I do not want anyone doing anything for me, so I gave a half-hearted smile and mumbled something about my finding it.

I reached the rear of the store and retrieved the hair spray, continually grumbling to myself that I still had to walk back to the car limping. My mind was racing as to how I could make the least spectacle of myself when a conversation penetrated my thoughts. I heard a woman's voice saying, "I don't know why, but I want to dye my hair one more time. It did not come out with the first treatment, but they say it might this next time."

I froze. Did I hear her right? She sounded so calm. I thought I was hurting, but I should be ashamed. This woman was losing her hair and was more collected than I was with a turned ankle!

I slowly traced behind their steps and eavesdropped on their conversation. She stated that the doctors had given her three months to live. She had lung cancer. It was found during a scan for kidney stones...

"Oh, God, I am sorry," was racing through my head. I was so absorbed with my perfect day's being ruined that I had failed to think of anyone but me. Here was a woman with the same length of time to live that I had to wait for my book to be published. To me, three months seemed like eternity. I want to hold my book in my hands now. However, to her, three months is tomorrow.

Something made me introduce myself and tell her I would be praying for her. I asked her if she were afraid. "No," she said, "I only cry when I think I'll not get to watch my grandbabies grow up."

"You must be so close to God," I added. "I cannot believe how strong you are. You seem so calm."

"Yes," she said, "I am very close to God."

"You may still be living when all of us are gone," I said, as I motioned to encompass the others around us. "God still performs miracles."

"I know," she stated. "I am just leaving it up to Him."

I have not been able to get this woman off my mind. That night I tossed in bed until I got up and put these thoughts on paper. She was a great blessing to me when I should have been a blessing to her. She showed me what a bad day is. It is not a twisted ankle, unpublished book, or shopping for clearance specials. A bad day is knowing you have been told you have three months to live, although you yearn to watch your loved ones mature, put down roots, and be strong enough to stand the winds of time after you are gone. You want to make sure they are not mushrooms but established Christians who are capable of turning a three month sentence into a blessing, just as you did.

If we never meet again and you lose your fight with cancer, your story will live on in this manuscript I am including in my book. Your story will inspire others just as it inspired me, but I truly pray that God will let you live and find this story. If we never meet again on earth, I am sure we will one day meet in heaven.

CPSIA information can be obtained at www.ICGtesting.com
Printed in the USA
LVOW041013170911

246716LV00001B/193/P